FROM THE LIBRARY OF

Mrs. Murphy

"While visiting Ireland and England, I was inspired by my research of the dragon in European mythology. Many royal families throughout Europe ruled under the banner of the dragon. The most famous was Arthur Pendragon, whose personal crest was **The Red Dragon**. To this day the banner of Wales features a four-legged red and gold dragon.

"Celtic stories suggest that dragons existed in the Land of 'Faerie.' They were part of a larger family of earth elementals who symbolized energy, power and immortality. The clash between old and new beliefs resulted in the myth of Saint George killing the dragon, which had come to represent the old nature religions.

"The Celtic knots in this book were inspired by seeing the Book of Kells, 900 AD, an ancient manuscript housed in Dublin's Trinity College Library."

Jody Bergsma

✠ ✠ ✠ ✠ ✠

DEDICATION

Dedicated to my dear friends, Rocky and Anna, and to all those who have "tamed their inner dragon," thus becoming successful rulers of their personal kingdoms.

SPECIAL THANKS

To Tiana Sanders for helping me write the first draft, Rocky Rockenbach for the second, Linda Marrian and Gail Smedly for proofreading, and John Thompson and the staff of Illumination Arts for their excellent editing.

DRAGON

Written and illustrated by
JODY BERGSMA

ILLUMINATION
Arts

PUBLISHING COMPANY, INC.
BELLEVUE, WASHINGTON

The first chill of autumn came swiftly to the Kingdom of Lugin. Bitter winds raced through village streets, scattering the leaves, while brilliant clouds danced before the approaching storm.

Within the castle, Briana, the fair young Queen, was about to give birth. Outside her door, King William paced restlessly. "How long must I wait!" he exclaimed. As lightning split the ominous clouds in the distance, the soft cry of a newborn babe was heard.

William rushed into the room, and Briana joyfully lifted the tiny boy to her proud husband. The King was tenderly holding his firstborn son when a white owl appeared on the window ledge and proclaimed,

"An heir to Lugin's crown is born; a fire bright shall be his throne.
To rule the Kingdom he is sworn; as Langilor shall he be known."

At the same time, in the Dark Forest east of Lugin, a beautiful green dragon nestled against a most unusual egg. The dragon clan gathered around her. They had never seen an egg so large, nor one that shimmered with such vibrant colors.

As the storm rumbled overhead, the shell cracked open, and a baby dragon struggled forth, stretching his glistening wings. The dragons gasped, for this

hatchling was unlike any other. He was the color of copper, of setting suns and autumn leaves. His eyes were like glowing embers.

Suddenly, a jagged bolt of lightning flashed into the forest lair, striking the infant as he voiced his first cry. All were astonished that he was unharmed. After a stunned silence, the new arrival was given the name, Saras.

As the years passed, the Kingdom of Lugin was blessed with peace and prosperity. Sheltered within the castle walls, Prince Langilor grew more slowly than other children. The young Prince loved the quiet of the royal garden, where he found peace with the animals and trees. Though he seldom spoke, Langilor played his mother's flute most skillfully, and he carried it with him

always. His sweet, innocent music and crystal-blue eyes could brighten the gloomiest day.

The King and Queen were very proud of their gentle son, yet some thought him too timid to be the future king.

Within the Dark Forest, the dragon clan lived in harmony with nature. As stewards of the land, the dragons protected the trees and rivers, and celebrated the changing of the seasons.

Living near the edge of the forest, Saras towered above the younger dragons and tormented them without mercy. He was swift and strong and terribly bold. While others tested their strength on land, he dreamt of flying. "Why do we

have wings if not to fly?" he challenged his mother.

"Put away your foolish dream!" she scolded. "The number of scales upon your back is the count of seasons since forest dragons have flown."

Saras began to practice in secret. One day, racing along a hilltop, wings fully spread, he caught an updraft and lifted off the ground. While the fearless young dragon soared above the treetops, other members of the clan watched in alarm.

On the Prince's ninth birthday, the entire court gathered for the celebration. The Royal Advisors, who feared that Langilor might never be strong enough to protect the Kingdom, gave him a small shield, a suit of armor, and weapons. King William's gift was a shimmering silver colt named Orion, for the constellation that rises with the autumn sky.

In the midst of the festivities, a luminous cloud filled the hall. A loud hum issued from the mist, and eight small men appeared, wearing tall hats that did not hide their pointed ears. Rhiannon, Queen of the elves who dwelt in the land of

Nagala, stepped out from her Guard of Eight. "Come forward, future King," she said gently. "We have brought you treasures."

The elfin guards presented the Prince with a silver bow and arrow, and a gold medallion inscribed "Choose Your Destiny." Then Rhiannon declared,

"A trial have you to prove your worth, to claim your throne and rights of birth. Your destiny is in your hand; through heart, the boy becomes a man."

Queen Rhiannon spoke again, "Always remember: This arrow will never miss its mark." With that, the Queen and her guards vanished into the cloud of mist.

In the heart of the forest, the Council of Dragons summoned young Saras. "We are displeased with your cruel treatment of the younger dragons. What say you for yourself?" Saras stood silently, his arms crossed and chin held high. "No apologies?" said the Dragon Master. "Then we decree that you be banished to Raven Mountain until you have changed your ways."

The defiant Saras vowed beneath his breath, "I will soon be more powerful

than any dragon! Ever!" Looking about for someone to bully, he chased a small squirrel, then swooped down to frighten a fawn. A curious crow flew by, and the dragon shouted, "Go away you ridiculous bird, or I will eat you!"

When the brazen crow teased Saras by pecking his tail, the angry young dragon roared with such ferocity that his breath turned to fire! As the flames singed the bird's feathers, a crafty smile crossed his face. "I am Saras, the fire-breathing dragon! Soon I will rule the entire forest. And the Land of Lugin, too!"

In the mornings Langilor studied diligently, but in the afternoons he loved to play his mother's flute and ride his silver colt, Orion. One day while the Prince was riding through the countryside, the Royal Advisors confronted King William. "Each week brings new threats from the Lords of the North," declared the eldest. "Yet Prince Langilor shows no interest in learning the ways of government and of war."

"He is ten years old and has yet to pick up his sword and shield," grumbled another. "How could he ever lead us in battle against our enemies?"

"And take away that ridiculous flute!" they all cried.

King William nodded sadly, for he knew he must consider the welfare of his Kingdom. And so, the Prince began to carry his sword while under the critical eyes of the Advisors. But sometimes, he would slip away to the garden, where he could play the flute in peace.

The Council of Dragons quickly gathered after hearing about the scorched crow. "Saras must be stopped," said the Dragon Master, "before the King orders death for the entire clan."

King William was indeed worried about the dangerous monster who was burning crops and frightening the people. A fire-breathing dragon was unheard of. And one that could fly! He ordered his knights to destroy the beast.

Each day Saras grew stronger. When the soldiers from Lugin approached, he would swoop down from the sky and char their armor with his scorching breath.

One night, Saras dreamt he was engaged in fierce battle with a young warrior. He returned the boy's bold stare and laughed, knowing he could crush this foe with one swipe of his tail. Yet the boy's bravery was formidable, and the piercing light from his blue eyes awakened Saras from his dream.

On mid-summer's eve of his twelfth year,
Langilor stood before his parents and the Royal Advisors,
who would judge his worthiness to be Lugin's future king.
His mother spoke first. "At his birth, the white owl
proclaimed that Langilor would be king. And remember
Queen Rhiannon's prophecy."

"An owl?" sneered the chief advisor. "If we listen to
elves and owls, the Kingdom will surely be lost. Are we not
threatened by a fire-breathing dragon and powerful enemies from
the north? The Prince must withdraw so that a suitable replacement
can be found."

Certain they were right, Langilor fled to the garden to hide his
tears. As the moon rose over the pond, he heard a mysterious voice,
"Conquer the dragon and claim your throne."

Looking about, the Prince saw only a graceful white swan.
"Go in search of the dragon alone," she said, "and you will
find the courage you seek." Then the swan disappeared, and
all that remained was moonlight glimmering on the water.

The next day, despite his fear, the Prince told his parents
about the swan's message. "I will conquer the dragon and prove
my worth!" he declared.

King William refused to consider such a foolish idea. "Even
my bravest knights cannot conquer this beast!" he sputtered.

Before sunrise the next day, Langilor arose and quietly collected his armor, sword and shield. Taking also his mother's flute and his silver bow and arrow, the young Prince rode bravely toward the Dark Forest, accompanied only by the white owl. On the outskirts of Lugin, children showered his path with flowers to show their love.

For three days and nights Langilor followed the dragon's blackened trail to Raven Mountain. Soon after beginning the rocky ascent, he shed his heavy armor, then the sword and shield. The path was treacherous and steep. When Orion failed his footing, the Prince set him free near a mountain stream. As the sun fell toward the western horizon, Langilor continued on foot, his every step mocked by the taunting cries of ravens.

Langilor wearily approached the smoking cave of Saras. Standing square before the dragon's lair, he set the silver arrow in his bow. Alerted by the ravens, Saras watched with amusement. "Think you, foolish Prince, to slay a dragon with just an arrow?"

"This arrow is magic, for it is a gift from the Queen of the elves," Langilor shouted. "Surrender now, or I know not what it may do!"

"Haaaa-a-a-a!" scoffed Saras. Fiery smoke billowed toward the young Prince, who responded by releasing his arrow. The silver missile bounced off the dragon's armored chest, off the rock wall, then back toward the Prince. In

a burst of light it struck the gold medallion protecting Langilor's heart, and he heard Queen Rhiannon's voice, "Now is the moment to choose."

With renewed courage, the Prince scrambled to a ledge above the cave. When Saras passed under the ledge, Langilor threw his cape over the dragon's eyes and bravely leapt onto his mighty neck.

Struggling to dislodge his enemy, Saras took flight. The furious dragon twisted blindly through the air, then lost his bearing and began tumbling head over tail toward the valley below. The ground rushed toward them at a terrifying speed, and they were swallowed by the night.

Langilor awoke in darkness, afraid that he had died. He struggled to move, but his entire body was wrapped in bandages. Then he heard a familiar voice. "I am still with you," said the white owl. "You are now safe in Nagala, the land of the elves."

When the wrappings were removed from his eyes, Langilor saw Queen Rhiannon standing before him. "Welcome, young Prince. Your visit is not unexpected, for this is part of your destiny."

Langilor was startled by an ominous rumble. Not far off, Saras was

struggling against his bonds, roaring with pain and frustration. "You alone must care for the great beast," said the Queen. "Know that as you heal the dragon, you will also be healing yourself."

Each day, the timid Prince brought food and water to the angry Saras. Each night he played his flute so beautifully that the melodies lingered in the dragon's dreams. As Langilor tended the dragon's wounds, his fear gradually began to dissolve. Saras now welcomed the boy's visits and even enjoyed Langilor's colorful stories, yet his need for freedom and open skies still called strongly.

Langilor spent most of his waking hours with the dragon. As days turned into weeks, Saras became stronger, and the young Prince grew more confident and self-assured.

The day finally came when the dragon knew he could escape. Testing the bonds that held him, Saras cautiously stretched his wings. Then, in one movement he snapped the chains, roaring in the glory of his freedom. Hearing the commotion, Langilor came running in time to see the mighty dragon preparing for flight. "Saras, don't go!" he shouted with all his strength.

The dragon hesitated, as he recalled the piercing blue eyes of the boy-warrior who had haunted his dreams. Suddenly, the scorched shell around his heart shattered, and the pain of lonely years fell away. Saras looked at Langilor and realized that he had made his first and only friend.

The next morning, a miraculous vision appeared through the mists of Lugin. A handsome young man was seen riding a huge, fire-breathing dragon. Alongside flew a white owl. The frightened villagers were amazed to hear Langilor's voice, "Do not fear. This is my friend, Saras the dragon. Send word to my parents that I am coming home."

With tears of joy, the King and Queen rode forth to greet their son. Long believing the Prince to be dead, the royal couple had been in deep mourning. Search parties had found only Orion, the scorched cape, and the discarded armor. Upon seeing Langilor astride the fearsome dragon, the entire court trembled in awe. Everyone, including the Royal Advisors, bowed deeply. King William

saluted. "Come away from the dragon, my son, and ride by my side. We will put this monster in chains and show your conquest to all the kingdom."

"Father," said the Prince, "we have no need for chains. The one who was an enemy has become a friend. I will enter the castle mounted on his back, as befitting the future king."

The story quickly spread. Visitors came from far and wide to honor the boy who had befriended the fire-breathing dragon. Fearing this wizard prince and his powerful new ally, the Lords of the North vowed to maintain friendly relations with Lugin.

In due time, Langilor became King. The townsfolk seldom saw the dragon, except at royal functions, or occasionally lighting up the night sky. But everyone knew that Saras lived in the royal garden and was Langilor's closest companion and protector.

The young King's resonant laughter and the music from his flute would often float over the castle walls. And whenever King Langilor withdrew from the company of men, people would whisper, "He has gone to be with the dragon."

And so it was that the spirit of fire was tamed
in a kingdom between the worlds,
and a new alliance began
between dragons and man.

P.O. BOX 1865, Bellevue, WA 98009
Tel: 425-644-7185 ✠ 888-210-8216 (orders only) ✠ Fax: 425-644-9274
liteinfo@illumin.com ✠ www.illumin.com

✠ ✠

Library of Congress Cataloging-in-Publication Data

Bergsma, Jody.
    Dragon / written and illustrated by Jody Bergsma.
    p cm.
    Summary: Born on the same night, a gentle prince and a fierce dragon find their destinies linked as they move toward fulfilling a prophecy that will affect the entire kingdom.
    ISBN 0-93-569917-1
    (1. Dragons Fiction   2. Fantasy.) I. Title
    PZ7B452235 Dr 1999
    (Fic)—dc21   99.25689
                                                                                 CIP

✠ ✠

Published in the United States of America

Printed by Tien Wah Press in Singapore

Book Designer:
Molly Murrah, Murrah & Company, Kirkland, Washington

THE ILLUMINATION ARTS COLLECTION OF INSPIRING CHILDREN'S BOOKS

ALL I SEE IS PART OF ME

By Chara Curtis, illustrated by Cynthia Aldrich $15.95   0-935699-07-4
Winner – Award of Excellence – Body Mind Spirit Magazine
An international bestseller. A child finds the light within his heart and his common link with all of life.

THE BONSAI BEAR

By Bernard Libster, illustrated by Aries Cheung $15.95   0-935699-15-5
Finalist – Best Children's Book – Coalition of Visionary Retailers
Issa uses bonsai methods to keep his pet bear small, but the playful cub dreams of following his true nature.

CASSANDRA'S ANGEL

By Gina Otto, illustrated by Trudy Joost $15.95   0-935699-20-1
Cassandra feels lonely and missunderstood until her special angel helps her find the truth within.

CORNELIUS AND THE DOG STAR

By Diana Spyropulos, illustrated by Ray Williams $15.95   0-935699-08-2
Winner – Award of Excellence – Body Mind Spirit Magazine
Grouchy old Cornelius Basset Hound can't enter Dog Heaven until he learns about love, fun, and kindness.

THE DOLL LADY

By H. Elizabeth Collins-Varni, illustrated by Judy Kuusisto $15.95   0-935699-24-4
The Doll Lady tells children to treat dolls kindly and with great love, for they are just like people.

DREAMBIRDS

By David Ogden, illustrated by Jody Bergsma $16.95   0-935699-09-0
Winner – Best Children's Book – Coalition of Visionary Retailers
A Native American boy searches for the elusive dreambird and its powerful gift.

FUN IS A FEELING

By Chara M. Curtis, illustrated by Cynthia Aldrich $15.95   0-935699-13-9
Find your fun! "Fun isn't something or somewhere or who. It's a feeling of joy that lives inside of you."

HOW FAR TO HEAVEN?

By Chara M. Curtis, illustrated by Alfred Currier $15.95   0-935699-06-6
Exploring the wonders of nature, Nanna and her granddaughter discover that heaven is all around us.

LITTLE SQUAREHEAD

By Peggy O'Neill, illustrated by Denise Freeman $15.95   0-935699-21-X
Little Rosa overcomes the stigma of her unusual appearance after discovering a diamond glowing within her heart.

THE LITTLE WIZARD

Written and illustrated by Jody Bergsma $15.95   0-935699-19-8
Winner – Best Children's Book – Coalition of Visionary Retailers
Young Kevin discovers a wizard's cloak while on a perilous mission to save his mother's life.

THE RIGHT TOUCH

By Sandy Kleven, LCSW, illustrated by Jody Bergsma $15.95   0-935699-10-4
Winner – Benjamin Franklin Parenting Award, Selected as Outstanding by the Parent Council Ltd.
This beautifully illustrated read-aloud story teaches children how to prevent sexual abuse.

SKY CASTLE

By Sandra Hanken, illustrated by Jody Bergsma $15.95   0-935699-14-7
Children's Choice Award – Children's Book Council
Alive with dolphins, parrots and fairies, this magical tale inspires us to believe in the power of our dreams.

TO SLEEP WITH THE ANGELS

By H. Elizabeth Collins, illustrated by Judy Kuusisto $15.95   0-935699-16-3
Finalist – Best Children's Book – Coalition of Visionary Retailers
A young girl's guardian angel comforts her to sleep, filling her dreams with magical adventures.

WHAT IF...

By Regina Williams, illustrated by Doug Keith $15.95   0-935699-22-8
Using his fantastic imagination, a little boy tries to delay bedtime as long as possible.

WINGS OF CHANGE

By Franklin Hill, Ph.D., illustrated by Aries Cheung $15.95   0-935699-18-X
A contented little caterpillar resists his approaching transformation into a butterfly.